Born in 1956, Joan Metelerkamp grew up in the midlands of Natal and was educated in Pietermaritzburg. After a post-graduate actor's diploma at UCT, she worked for a while in educational theatre in Cape Town and Pretoria before returning to English Studies. She has taught English at the Universities of Natal and the Western Cape. She now lives outside Durban with her husband and two children. Her first volume of poetry, *Towing the Line,* was joint winner of the 1991 SANLAM literary award for an author previously unpublished in book form.

By Joan Metelerkamp:

Towing the Line - a volume of poetry in *Signs : Three Collections of Poetry.*

Stone
No More

The birth of Aphrodite, Ludovisi Throne (Terme Museum, Rome)

Joan Metelerkamp

Gecko Books
1995

STONE NO MORE

Poems by Joan Metelerkamp

Text © Joan Metelerkamp 1995

ISBN: 1-875011-07-2

First Published 1995
Gecko Books cc
21 Hereward Rd
Umbilo, Durban, 4001

Photograph of the author by Paul Weinberg
Design and desktop publication by Susan Andrews
Printed by Kohler Carton and Print (Natal).

For Michael, with love.

Acknowledgements are due to *New Coin* and *New Contrast,* in which some of these poems first appeared. Thanks to Robert Berold and Ingrid De Kok for their editorial comments. "*Poem for my mother*" won third prize for the 1992 Sydney Clouts Memorial Prize for poems published in *New Coin.* "*After the Interview*" and "*For Davydd*" were published in *Like a House on Fire* (Cosaw 1994). "*Birth of Venus*" has recently appeared in *Carapace* (Vol 1, No 1).

Thanks to Tony Voss and to Gertrud and Peter Strauss for their generous response to these poems and to Gertrud and Peter and Veronica Klipp for seeing them into print.

CONTENTS

At the centre you sit

in your old gym-slip
looking at me -

it could be my mother
could be my daughter
but it is you

(for I am named for you).

You sit schoolgirl
frowning up at me
smiling wanting to know

what it is I want of you.

In other photographs
you are dressing up -
the great actor you

never were (nor was my mother
nor I.)

You are only ten
and you are smiling
yes? yes? you ask

what is it as I stand

before the brink sealed before
your ageless aging -

buried in the furrow
on your forehead harrowed
between my mother's brows
between mine.

What can I say
I hover in the wings
you have centre stage sun

bright Rosalind brave Joan
shining on your daring
your sword;

for forty years

rooted in the shadow
of pre life

I have waited in the wake
of your act

but it is I, I who
must go on
speaking now:

"Let no man mock me
for I will kiss her ....
Come;
I'll fill your grave up: stir; nay, come away ...."

(For my grandmother
who committed suicide in 1951)

Self / Critic

1 Birth of Venus

Unscrupulous Athena! marking with the patriarchal pen,
mastered so surely in your fine hands, mistress of Authority,
defender in the name of women's rights the father's legal rites,
decreeing what I write, my heart's hard passion forming, "outrageous",
"illegitimate", "reductionist", "wrong": not quite contemptible,
even you could not stoop so low; you have had your say, go batter
other Arachnes now whose weaving you fear might not (might) match yours.

Lady! you might not have reckoned on Aphrodite!   Wait - I am
rising out of my shell, and when my bleak anger has fallen off
in scales around my feet - new-skinned, armourless - Athena, I shall
greet you there, where you reflect the sun in hard-forged, brilliant shield
raised toward the light, bravely defending your territory, I shall
venture in unsolicited, insouciant, shameless in my home
made shawl, home spun words, appliquéd with paisleys, diamonds, satin
stitched with floribunda roses, such warp and weft of words, such drapes
of greens, vermillions, falling round my naked form like hair like flax
like gold, protecting me like women's arms, waiting, on the shore, receiving me, wrapping me in finest textures of their craft, patterns
of women's work, from sea to sea, from here to then, from knot to knot,
no gleaming sword ripping through, no ink black spots struck across my words,
nor even the distorted reflection in your shield, will destroy.

2 Medusa

Polished words strung along precisely weighted syllabic lines
distilling the fury I'd felt for years to fierce stones - a string,
I felt, glinting - like Granny's necklace in the dark like the lights
of Maritzburg below, seen for the first time through the mist from
World's View, as we drove through the night ...

                                 (fearing you so long, Lady,
this self same Medusa, bearing your Word, lead, stone in the womb,
sharpening my pencil against the whet-stone of your judgement,
etching the rim, cold surface forming the opaque polished-stone
looking glass, *"look I can face you now critic, whom do you see there,
whose familiar face is that you see?"*)

                                 They sent the poem back:
"the subject is too viewed from the outside; enact it better."
Years, years, internally, silting galling sediment to stone;
voyeurs: take it, use the object, slay the subject if you dare!

After the interview

Outside, outside the window, the delicious
monster waving to me, drowning, naming the
parts, inadequately - this is the worksheet -
gesturing, just above the learned men's heads,
its grotesque, glossy-leafed, serrated-fingered
comfort of indifference - while I, giving lip
service to what philosophic cornerstones
I was not sure, shoved the good ground for poems
for their benefit into the corner of
the syllabus - what place can poetry have -

from hidden depths the word did surface like a
bubble carried on the desperate current
of my mind, quivered, little green tendrils, un-
admitted: "poems"; I shut it out (or could
it have been "joy"? or perhaps, perhaps "pleasure"?)

through my choked throat (passages of inner ears
burning like hot bottled chillis from the not
so fortuitous coral flaming virus)
I couldn't say, but I should have said, something
about poetry in all its multiple
convoluting manifold forms opening
up against hegemonic popular texts
(the relationship of content, liquid, os-
mosing with the reader's structures of feeling,
to the permeable, malleable form;

like the wild rooted ficus pushing against
the four brick walls with all its might squeezing not
a brick out of place?)
I should have said something to do with thinking
it a worthwhile organism of shifting
meanings, contradicting, transforming, meanings -

I should have said, in the face of your odd self-
effacement, your equivocation, about the
Legitimacy of English Studies, can
one decolonise the mind or overturn
colonial history (man harrowing
clods) by doubting relevant grounds for it here?
The World Bank does not conduct its empire in
Zulu (nor does Mandela for that matter
but how much a flaming red herring is that?)

Empowering students: that was the buzz phrase
and how was I thinking of empowering
students - to do what - I didn't ask - to read
to overturn the world run by IBM?

Drifting past, a straw, the question of gender
and I missed the moment to seize it, to talk
of power; too busy flirting with power
of the Institution, Authority,
too busy longing for Legitimacy,
Recognition from The August to be looked
at by the elders and seen for what I am.

Up through the porous surface keeping night from
day, words from meanings, seeds from forms, came the dream
could it be this bland faced man was the one I
was dancing with - illicit delicious fling-
ing of our bodies to each other - but I
always dance better with naked shameless feet
I replied to the other woman, angry,
proprietorial, territorial
put your shoes back on and leave my man alone ⸴

o the nocturnal dance with Authority
was delicious, but illicit, illicit;

not for me the power to fraternise with
the heady men; mine the space in the margins,
mine the place outside the high ceilinged rooms, the
spare necessity of turning underground
flirtation with verse to a marked out space of
diurnally tillable soil for digging
on my own with my pen, yes, for gathering
in me seeds for nurturing wild words for growth.

Trees Sky Space

"hope not being hope
until all ground for hope has
vanished" - Marianne Moore

until you find yourself functioning
in a rhythm of forgetfulness,
not bothering to glance up at the
clouds streaking crepuscular cerise
across blue, through the bathroom window,
above sweaty hay-heads of your kids;

until you find yourself head down to
routine repetition, no glimpse of
recreation, world recreating
itself in quotidian spleandour,
neighbour's wild strelizia dancing
with masked weavers, flying to plunder
meticuluously, strip by strip, your
bamboo, outside the bathroom window,
head to tail, squadrons darting, black, gold,
getting houses in order for chicks,
so intent they do not notice you
notice them through the bathroom window;

until you forget to keep looking,
keep taking joy, until you feel your
muscles seize down your back with bending,
you forget why poems bother to
celebrate restoring movement, trees
sky space.

When you ask me

*"We move, but our words stand
become responsible
for more than we intended
and this is verbal privilege"* - Adrienne Rich

When you ask me
but have the mothers shifted
meaning in their mothering

how can I say
yes unequivocally
when as you tell me the words

the literature
the documentation the
records answer no the myths

remain intact
mothers receive meaning they
don't shift meaning images

Mary Mother
of Forgiveness Plenitude
Effacement Loss Mother Earth

Mater Mama
Afrika I counter yes
yes we are living with these

mothers slowly
inserting ourselves into
interstices of routine.

Poem for my mother

Like Anne Sexton's daughter, long ago
I called on God
                    knows what, something some-
one else instead of you:
                              finally
having fallen from the horse that dragged
me, head hit by hooves like coconuts
clapping with every galloping pace,
finally
            having gathered up your
daughter like a fallen pod,
                                  having
watched her dragged by the demented horse,
finally
            held to your heaving breast,
sensing your staggering shock I
                                      asked
if I wasn't too heavy for you;

only seven, holding the secret
of separation so tight, it seems,
seamed to my breast, over seasons of
years, that even now the unclean, the
ambiguous, severing of selves,
mother and daughter, sears through my love.

Undercurrents

My most underworld unexpressed love
my tongue struggled to articulate -
three sharp words I love him

brazened their inefficacy - white
light turned on the clandestine coupling:
this is no love for day-

light, the words said, inadmissible
as the leaf-in-wind whispered secrets
of genesis, forests

where amphibians heave back to breast,
tendrils stir, limbs strewn across shoulders
breathe, as though the sun though

shining then seldom shone through to there.

Gawain, green knight, your head chopped off, off
trail for a while, where could our love lead?
The word love now written

between us I wanted to write but
it is my declaration again
raising the head of that

grave doubt hovering moth-like round me;
did love ever enter for you or
the Lady of Shallott

was I punting the river alone?
(Too far back it would take me too deep?)
Merciful, protective

fear ebbed the current locked the tongue like
Philomel's before, like Pandora's
box sprung open, it burst

joy's grape before it turned

to soured wine of failed saviours;
instead, the sweet fruit enclosed in un-
conventionally green

armour of an outsize pineapple
awkward as an armadillo I
brought to your dark door-step;

and whispering secrets in the dark,
behind us in the house, two small boys
your son and his friend gave

room to our awkward words, flapping round
the white bright kitchen light, wings tracing'
desire's subtext, hushed.

But still this undertow;

for all I know about this love now
is that deep in oceanic dreams
it swims to haunt the cave

(the watery grave) the womb lick the
sleeping libido to blue wet flame.

For Davydd

All along the highway
breaks were burning and fiery brands -
aloe candelabra -
marching in full flower against the
July sky defying the dust, smoke

and dust filtering memories of
chilhood, returning to school, weekly
sabbath nostalgia, familiar dip,
modulation of melancholy -
the palpable un-nameable shade;

all along the highway
- Durban to Maritzburg -
on this recent Sunday
thoughts of adolescence
sift too through familiar
dust and thrusts of aloes
flaming against the blue;

déjà vu - the party
when we arrived there took

me back to a slightly later time:
the awkward budding of adulthood -
long winter afternoons we spent then
drinking wine in the sun on the grass -

always something missing always the
bruises of longing: or sharper still
cold fear beneath the warm skin,
midday sunshine shrouding winter's bite;

speaking of old friends, lost
friends, she sat on the step
with her wine, in the sun,
reminding me of time,
time before our children:

the lost friend: his absent
face between us, clearly:

"I saw him in London;
he is so thin" she said
"his coat hangs here" (pointing)
"shoulders here" (contracting
his powerful frame to
the pathetic points of
collar bones) "and no hair;"

- dust and the sun and the cold
panic restrained - keeping face -

you with your huge iconoclast's laugh -
long gone - unsuitable wild love for
a man who could never really love
a woman, would turn to other men,
any one could see that then, but me ...

come before me as at first - upturned
flash of face, bearded, curls; and huge limbs;
hammering the set for the Dada -
and me, gauche slip of a first year flung
about the stage - the mirror wardrobe -
my eyes only for you even in
Afrikaans - "Poppie, wat het daardie
man langs jou wat ek nie het nie ..." -

(the story I was learning by heart:
"with despair - cold, sharp despair - buried
deep in her heart like a wicked knife ...")

you taught me how to look
at hills and see lines flow,
you taught me how to look
at lines and see hills, from
World's View to Maritzburg
the purple wooded hills
after rain jellied with
colours of your glazes;
female forms reclining;

from the mould of my face
you formed a Greek godess:

three masks, three faces I think there were:

one, a pod form opening, folding
like the next, cracking and imploding;

barely discernable features, squashed,
through the birth, to the third shape pure face
beauty I dared not recognize, mine;

young goddess, I could not look at you
then could not see myself as he saw
me could not love myself with his love

could not feel that stone face kept mine
knew the shards it did not show bitten deep
the cry it silenced the shrieking girl
flung across his bed - his house entered -
forced herself - the gap above the door ...

metamorphosing shapes you replaced
with totemic phalluses you formed
to ward off death, keeping doubt at bay?
thrusting poles - eagle like vulture like
heads, set about with feathers and beads;

(who did they stand for then, what did they
see - the garish peacocks of fashion
the Art World, Rivonia style?)

Subversive stoic, far away, cold;
bearing the burden of your illness
alone, refusing compassionate inquiry,

refusing (from friends' accounts) to share
more than the eloquent shape, sight of
yourself,
> I cannot see you from here;
from Durban to London the silence
has fallen; the letter I wrote
lies unsent: if I may not write of
your death,
>> how can I face you at all?

Joan

1

Spirit and Freedom:
two potent metaphors
for me to define;
you send me home with them,
healing women, you
offer them to me:
how can they be mine?

In shape of my own life,
what has been, what would
have been, what would I
have had be?
                        What is
the shape, lurks in the dark,
hides in the shade, cries
in the night, longs for
the child, longed for a child,
long, for the child, waiting;

(poetry, reading poems, making
poems a way of life, was second,
a substitute; now the play between
covering the loss the spectre of
freedom has left and recovering

the trace, that heart heard of, ghost guessed; can
poetry bear spirited freedom?)

2

Thinking of the women's words,
gift to me of metaphors
for me to define myself,
this morning, in the shower,
running water running,
down the body, streaming,
streaming down, the body
bowed under the flowing
words, pouring words, in me,
over me, out of me,
grandmother's words come to me:

"O George if you had dancing in the blood
  like I do ..."

(in a letter, just before her marriage,
words to George hot with love, pouring delight,
beating, beating with love like a promise).

3

She lay on the carpet.
George tearing the snippet
of wallpaper, lampshade
marking it with a cross:
this was where the bullet
tore through; his words in his
historian's careful
lettering intricate
stitching over the gap,
in the album, amongst
the family letters
faithfully assembled,
bequeathed to Wits archives.

Breathe, breathe deeply spirit
gasping to the surface.

In memory of Joan
Rose-Innes Findlay, rest,
in peace, spirit, leaving

the gap to be borne, stone
weight,
         mother
                 images
all borne with me all, all
of my life nothing new
to discover now but

let the soft grief force its
way up, breath of air out,
inadmissible cry
stroke the quiver the core
feather arrowing shoot.

4

Words like arrows sent now
words return me to task;
if you had dancing in
the blood ...

spirit and freedom you profound abstracts
how you are lodged in the marrow of self,
how is your coming together in me?

spirit sweet as sex dancing in the blood
knowledge death and life sweet as sex freedom

What were the men in our lives to be
for us, grandmother, mother and me?

to recover the child
to allow the child room
to dream to learn to be?
give the child room to be.

Mothers were there to give the child room.

Mothers carried the can. When she died
when she shot herself the message to
my mother was: your turn now - carry
the can, not I not any longer.

Heavily heavily heavily
we bear it: the shelter, the liquid
spirit for the child's roots, their green shoots;
caritas, caritas lacrimae.

5

To go on, how go on, go on
leadenly threading the life-line,
seeming snapped now, of words like red
beads spilling like blood on the ground.
Words, words flow over me, drowning.

Taking myself out of the house
to think, I have come here to think
how to thread together scattered
shards of our lives - seeking comfort
I have come now to public space

and find this macabre mirror-sharp everyday
mall of getting and spending, where nothing
is authentic nothing is worth knowing

nothing is admissible, uncivil
centre, aetiolation of friendlessness,
glossy women from another climate
made-up for combatting the elements
as well as each-other, people this place
invites me to despise, barely veneered
back-fangs of capital, you gangrenous
Musgrave, severed from the life-line of trees
trichilia emetica outside.

Freedom: to overturn the black iron
pseudo art-deco tables, to live in
a city integrated, some how, some
way, the shops interfacing with the trees,
the street, people, not facing each other
in a self-inturning self-consuming
waste, laying waste our powers: this city
has had its vegetation, once wild, its
one recommendation, almost destroyed.

People destroying their life-blood.
Suicide.

To keep the spirit dancing
in the blood.

6

She was the secretary
to the communist party.
(How much dancing there?)

The atom bomb for freedom
Stalinism in Russia
Nationalism here;

and then their listing; blight of
the land we list you; blighted
to the root of your

mothering, blight bequeathed to
her children, inheritors
of her shattered world

a month after their listing she shot herself.

Child, little girl, alone,
unknown father, Donald,

dead in the seige of Mafeking;
English mother, Alice, angel
in the too-bright alien sun

nursing others always
the ailing, the fallen.

Little girl, three
(like her great-grandaughter, my daughter, now -
in you Frances, "free-woman", I see her
portraited face, or is it the snap of
mother frowning over flower-picking?)
little girl, passed,
precious parcel,
from family
to family;
alone, alone
soft at the core,
brave chin, brave, brave
chinny-chin chin.

soldiers of christ arise and put your armour on

So who is responsible
comrades, let the blood spill
on the floor, spirit seeping?

I know who gathers it in,
fills the can, still, carries it:

mother appealed to, at the age of
individuation, crucial time
dancing in her blood, seeking to let
it free: ("don't go out this afternoon,
stay, stay here with me.")

I know the scene too well to recreate
it is old - what was I trying to say?

Freedom,comrades responsibility
individual individuation -

Image of community severed at the core:
where were you espousing freedom community
solidarity, did you turn your backs to her
bleeding on the floor? where were you, Oupa George,
wrangling for justice, dreams failing, finding comfort
from another woman;
                                        self-aggrandisement
and power; the fine difference between them and
self-love, the struggle for self-empowering love.

7

They gave me "spirit" and "freedom"
eight women in the room with me
each hesitantly revealing
herself, the others, tears rising
falling - praxis begins at home.

The weight of pain rolling
the stone of Sysiphus
gathering momentum
hard, hard as a phallus
knocking breath out of me,
this is the centre, the core.

I will no longer hide
their pain.
I will put down
the sword.
I shall not defend
their pain.
I will not mother
loss.
I will not nurture
pain.
O Joan
Joan Rose-Innes Findlay
where are you now
where does your broken spirit lie?

8

Women, I wanted to write you
an elegy to our pain;
feeling no poet I made
muffins instead: telling you,
telling you I long to make
a poem for you to use
the fabric of words to weave
a wonderful shroud for our loss.

I longed for you to take it,
to rub it through your fingers

feeling its fine stuff, passing
it from one to the other,
holding it up to the light,
laying it in the centre

there letting it be
a symbol of peace

carried within us
its message healing.

Stitch, stitch gently over the gaping flesh
cover the wound keeping the life blood in;

I, I, and the knocking on the door
in the dark the dark man in the dark
admit it, admit it.

He is my free spirit
the lover in the dark
is my own spirit come

to embrace me
yes it is he
he will lift me
into his arms
he will bear me:
terrible weight

the dark god
my own psyche
shall bear.

Ah - I see who he is now!
is this what it looks like
is this my dream lover
bearing me freedom is
this who my spirit is?

how he has called to me called to me
thus i and the woman calling
cried in the dark night after night
waiting for me dreaming of me
saying that now he is not as
he was but all to me all of me.

(love thyself: soldiers of Christ arise)

What does he look like?
whispers pass as if

over a new born child
ah he is beautiful

he shines he has protean
forms let him be now he will

reveal himself to me again
I carry him in me let me

warm him carry him softly a seed
a bean a seed in a healing pod.

Love in the first fling
lets dancing in the blood
let this be love as strong
as love for my children
love of life struggling
sustaining despite
daily discomfort,
letting love here shoot
green tendrils through the
familiar ground the
imperfect terrain
that is.

Space of the Imagination

1

The exile has come to stay;

a brief reprieve from inevitable
separation;
days, we walk, talk, sit in the suburb: sun,
strelizia,

weaver's pendulous nests, erithrina,
dust; nights, skin-deep
sleep, never enough to let the muscle
go, let alone

the marrow. Nights:
separate dreams
persistent whisps
of private scenes
from other lands
from other times:

straws above sleep
like Lawrence's mother's hair on his shirt
like smoke after a cigarette, linger.

Knowing he would be gone soon, I told him,
the exile, my longing to write my dreams;
tunnel at the end of the light, he quipped.

What of you layered away in there what
longing for you
is when it is,
if it is what
metaphor you are for me what power
you have for me
why; curious
this symbol of desire why does it
take your form, the
day-night porous sun-seeped hair-shirt of you;
dream secreted
discreet secrets strewn up, beached
bleached in the sun.

Dream 1: I shall
come to; dream 2:
I shall come to
dreams 3 4 5
and 6 I shall
come to again -

you, before me, laughing, the laugh I have
missed in me, I
have lost you, love

what I have lost in me made me feel me
like you, laughing.

The exile said realise the bottom line,
the bottom line:
one is one and all alone and ever
more shall be so.

Later he said loneliness is not so
terrible; there are always things to do:
walking along South Beach, for example,
he said, picture
being able, precisely, to describe
the sky (above
the bluff, dry, dry,
sand showing through
the bush, the moon,
high, high, the smog
sinking in stripes, meeting sea, e.t.c.)

2

Today the exile and I went to lunch
at your house. Today I watched you moving
in your kitchen, among specific pots,
there, preparing our pranzo al fresco:
you, figure of my dreams, telling your son,

not to open the new cheese, finish the
old. So there you are, you too, the pater
familias, bearing your abrasive
rules for the young, the desirous, the bold;

monosyllabic I sat at your lunch

for Eros made me crumble,
laughing, lounging,
Eros, Eros lay crumpled,
like a rose.

Pranzo al fresco: this is no country
of the heart, no
this is Manor Gardens, Cato Manor,
Mayville, "life-style", a means of survival,
imprisoning the passions of the heart.

"Well, I love it" the iconoclast claimed -
cupid's bull's-eye -
from your verandah we looked out to raw
eczema of virulent match-boxes,
new housing, spreading on the dry-skinned hill:

"I love it," she said again, "for years I've
been looking at this empty hill, for years,
and all those people without houses and
now it's being **used**;"

arrow: to the heart
of dreams that people
might make their own room
for housing their own
growth; instead, quick
results, quick buck;
quick, green, desire
deracinated;

(and squatting, lying low, cheek by jowl,
in the interstices of the bush, houses.)

"Speaking of housing ..." from another guest
describing dimensions of her vacant
flat; and we, tipping our hats at crumpled
Eros, passed platitudes of what one might
make, two might, in

an empty flat.
Eros kept me
quiet, unable to come with it straight:
can I please have your flat for a woman
fleeing Folweni; please may Fortunate
Siyabonga, Nkosimpile, enter ...

imagined, illicit love-making, locked
my tongue (sex, said
the exile, is made of two elements:

imagination and friction - meaning
bits of bodies rubbing) imagining

the bits of bodies rubbing in the free
zone of the flat, how could I fill it with
pressing human need? (Beggars at the gate
the exile had long-last seen; a sing-song
repertoire in the name of Jesus we
are crying on you we are so hungry.)

3

Seventh dream: image from the exile's film
about film-making; birds reeling into
the sky, high, between framing gothic greys;
arches bordering imagination
limitless space.

If I ran I could catch up with you
and run I did
if I ran I could go with you
so run I did

and in the immigration office I
was saying "yes, I have enough, I can
bring in enough,
look, I have two live chickens for supper;"

cut to: birds reeling high, the sky between
buildings lining the medieval street;

birds in the infinite air;

then you got up,
across the passage, motioning yourself,
and my saying "yes, yes, I am coming"
(if you don't mind)

but you had left

4

the exile gone

departed all the guests
petals full blown
lying limp
reflected on the surface of the dark
rose eros rose eros ...

Portrait

Morning. The woman moves about her house,
opens the doors evenly, lets in the sun -
aura of ease, this morning, plenitude,
grace; here she is assured of her place.

Inside: she knows her privilege well;
from the french doors on the east she moves
along the passage toward the west -
beyond the open-plan living-room
wild strelizia, the courtyard wall.

Her hair is brown, bobbed, fired by the sun,
smooth as a seal from the sea, seeming
oiled. She is dressed in moss-green striped
with indigo - a kimono, though
this is Durban, the Berea.

It is a warm November Saturday.
The morning is here. She lets in the light.
Chelmsford Road. She knows its contradictions
well: towards the dip, thorny many-stemmed
chatachme aristata; umkhuhlu;
albizia; and, over the tended
park, mango trees bearing stringy fruit
the refugees have been wheeling away
in orange pockets, in shopping trolleys,

down the swept suburban street,
residents safe as houses behind their walls.

Saluting the trees, she turns back
through her house, reaching her hand out,
absently, for familiar shapes
(her mind drifting, retina of inner
eye reflecting dappled shiftings; the warm
and cold of the undercurrents sifting).

On the counter-top, between the kitchen
and the dining room table (used for work),
on the counter-top: a porcelain cone;
flawless white supported by gnarled struts like
tree trunks whose angles, whose texture, movement,
fired in clay, bear effort, like ant-like
slaves, human arms, backs, dragging stone slabs to
erect geometrical perfection,
pyramids, art of death in desert sands;
pure cone, buttressed by privilege, by sweat;
artifact made by a friend for a dead
friend; artifact, artist, elegiac
gesture, separate only in her work,
her criticism, the daily arts page,
but here, here, an object, simply, and loved.

This is her weekend of reprieve, of work -
children and husband are briefly away -
see - she should be quite alone, to think
of the reviews she must write, and perhaps,

perhaps to paint. But if you are quiet
you will become aware there is a child
here somewhere in the house - a refugee:
she is on the north stoep with her water
colours; look carefully the child might seem
her own - the same seal sleek hair seeming oiled
by the sun.   The child sits on the grass mat
on the slowly warming floor; her skirt
stretches across her knees, one raised at right
angles to the other. She looks up - round
eyes alert - then returns to the picture
at hand. Refugee, not from Folweni
but from the privilege of boarding school,
thrust on the woman by the bondage of
school-girl friendship: the child's mother her best
friend. So; where the woman should be here alone
there are two, alone, with shadow figures.

This morning, shadows of forms felt pressing
simultaneously - like her cone's struts
from different angles thrusting toward the
centre: the dead ceramicist to whom
her cone is dedicated; a painting,
someone else's, from those she must review;
the child; Mamaké's flight from Folweni -
("we slept last night in a ditch, outside, we
were too afraid to stay inside the house")
what dreams, what dreams can you have in ditches -
the dark man; her own painting (pleasure of

spaces - non verbal relationships - paint);
but to give each element its place, to
trace, find its influence on the others.

The ceramicist: friend of the woman
who made the cone - are the struts to the cone
a quotation of his work - like the poles,
rising totems, his feathered skulls on poles,
sceptres warding off the spectre of death;
the shock of his voice, taped, before he died -
aspirant, agonised - how to draw breath -
ripples and ripples and ripples of cold
through her skull, after the call, when he died -
"it's only something physiological
that's happened to someone you haven't seen
for a long time, somewhere, far away" -
her husband's voice jolting her from shock then.

(I am five or six, I am dreaming
I am lying in a ditch, I know
where it is, it is under the hedge,
the dairy, a snake has bitten me
I am sinking I cannot move my
limbs I cannot call I am dying
Egypt dying no-one can help me
when I am dead I will suffocate
I will be buried, buried alive.)

The child: cocooned in politeness and
low-grade misery, like a virus.

The woman will move out to the stoep now
to where the child is painting; she takes her
coffee with her, sits down in the cane chair.
The child glances up, smiling - a social
requisite - then eyes back to her painting.
The woman will wait. She is unburdened
by hurry or responsibility.
It is an ease, a distance, a gap of
silence not often shared with her children.
She rests her feet on the small blackwood stool -
figures of the dead banished by the gold
and black darting forms, masked weavers, bursting
high, through the neighbour's wild strelizia.

The child is eating her roll, reaches for
it absently, chews as she dips her brush.
The silence holds them - together, apart.

"Look" she says, and brings the woman her work.
It is a giraffe. The woman does not
say lovely darling I like your yellow.
The giraffe, wild, primitive, magic as
a totem. "Have you seen a real giraffe?"
she asks. "No; this is a magic giraffe."
"I can see that - I see it is wild
and still simultaneously, alert."
"It is waiting." "What is it waiting for?"
"For its mother - she's there - far away;
she's left this little giraffe here because
she's frightened of lions."

                    Her hand reaches
out to stroke the child's hair - it cannot;
it does not reach.
                         "Shall I paint too?" Kneeling
down, she takes a brush, dips it carefully.

They are sketching together with charcoal
in the courtyard; they haven't bothered to dress.
She is sketching; shorthand; notes for painting;
a huge albizia stretches across
the page; under it, a mother, in wide
soft straw hat and diaphanous dress raised
by the breeze, reaching through the long grass
to a child. "Why hasn't she got any
hands," asks the child; and the child, why hasn't
it got any feet? It raises one knee
toward her, showing its calf. Is it hurt?
Is it dancing? Has something bitten it?

(The dark man, stroking her, stroking her leg -
the dark man, familiar stranger, stroking -
see, I have roused you, your nipples are up -
and she calling, come, come, into me, come
am I not ready for you, dark man? No
I am not ready for you, see, I am not
erect: the phallus, limp substitute, loss.

dark man dream man
why do you come
to remind me

of loss, what is
this desire what hole does it
burn, what can I
not shore up?)

It is Saturday. She should be working;
here she has been given the space between
domestic duties - even the child sits
quietly sketching - why has she put down
her charcoal, to let in dreams?

The painting,
subject of her critical attention:

in front: two cupids, two cherubs, handles
of a stone urn, dipping to the purples,
petunia pinks, carefully contained.
Behind: precise criss-cross of growth, garden
of grandeur, Versailles or Vaux-le-Viconte.
Two cupids, two cherubs, nosing
into flowers in full bloom heads in the
blossom laughing, see, ever-lastingly-
stone heads may touch behind the flowers, see
if we can kiss! Foregrounded, the detail,
the classically marginal - Eros
in corners, cherubs on ceilings; lurking
in the background, the old order, strong lines,
aristocracy, geometry, wealth.
And all in a gilt frame - purple framed in gold -

culture, cultivation, inheritance
breeding, money, art; Eros, Eros, growth.

If you were an artist
you could bring the abstracts
into relationship
without logic, without
connectors, with spaces,
with shapes, with gestures, with
colours instead of text,
context, and words words words.

She would have to find something to say: South
African artist in France, paints sculptures -
grey, formal, heroes - quotes Europe to re-
shape its forms, ironically? reverently?
Claims his inheritance, European
Art: smallest painting darting colour to
my critic's eye, my mother's, lover's, heart;
breath to dead stone, form of flesh, breath blown from
corners, erotic cherubs, like the wind
blown into the paintings of old masters.

The child has stopped drawing.
Head in her hand she sits,
bruises under her eyes.

woman: Why have you stopped? You were doing so well.
child: It's boring.
woman: Is it? I thought you were enjoying it.

child: I'm drawing boring things.
woman: Are you really? What do you want to draw?
child: That's the point, it's all dull.
woman: That's a pity. I liked your last drawing.
child: But maybe not this one.
woman: But why not? I can't see why I shouldn't.
child: Because this one's of me.
woman: But that sounds like a lovely idea!
child: Do you really think so?
woman: Yes! I want to see how you see yourself.
child: But this is a funny
    picture because it's me
    thinking and I don't know
    how to draw me thinking
    and it may be boring.
woman: But who would it be boring for? For whom?
child: For my friends, and teachers.
woman: But must they see? Must you show it to them?
child: Of course I must! It must
    be a proper showing
    picture like the ones you
    look at so carefully
    and then you write about.
woman: Well it will be. It will be "Self-Portrait".
child: My teachers won't like it.
woman: Really not? What do you think they would like?
child: Doing pictures; things that
    have happened. And places
    we have been to;
    sometimes our family,

50

and people that matter.
woman: I think maybe you're shy. Do you think so?
child: Yes, and they won't like it.
woman: And that will feel as though they don't like you?
child: I want them to like it.
woman: You haven't begun. Why don't you begin?
child: But it's so much work - it
        may be a waste of time.
woman: I know; it's so much work to do the things
        you want to do - why is it so much work?

this dark man: no wonder the phallus
was limp - little slave, how will you
erect the cone, the pyramid, the shape?

If I could paint, if I could paint anything
is the chair a legitimate subject or
my children's faces? Dark man, shall I paint you -
and here comes the painting master's ruler down -
in how many attitudes shall I paint you
and whose shape do you have? Rodin's thinker or
the sandy-haired man, all my dream men changing
shape? And who would hang you? Where? The hanging man,
upside-down, signifying indecision.

Steadfast man, stumbled upon in my dreaming:

        I'm limping
So I see.
        Who are you?

Me? The man you've been looking for.
            The helmet maker?
The shining man.
            What are you doing here?
I will help you jump.
            What is there down there?
Women, selling their wares; baskets, beads, grass mats,
pyramids of mangoes, hands of bananas;
intricate work fringing the plastic tat, hats
saying "Durban" made in Taiwan; sweat, dust ...
            Have you been here long?
Marking time; keeping guard for the king.
            Who is the king?
I serve him only; his word is law ...
            I want the password ...
Wanting the Word has given you that limp.
Jump. Jump. I'll carry you if you like, see ...
            how strong you are, sweaty man, yes I see.
You are afraid of after we have jumped?
            You might stop listening; grow weak, flabby.
I shall show you how to recognise me:
take off your clothes: let me ...
            take off your clothes.

The child sharpens her pencils.
She will dip their coloured tips
in the cool water; let them
drink their fill - take them
like brushes dripping with paint.

"Desiring the phallus" means entering
the realm of the symbolic: do my dreams
mean I have entered? Desiring the phallus
is the condition of the symbolic;
which is language, is it using "the phallus"
or is it "desiring the phallus"?
Having entered, can one never arrive?
How **use** language then - desiring the phallus -
how can it substitute loss, then, desire:
what is there to use to plug up the hole,
what instrument, what presence, what pen, then?

What is your shape dream man in whose presence
desire is pleasure and even, waking,
longing to prolong the bruise of your absence?

Your shapes: half-turned, crouched, like Rodin's Thinker,
while I, I weave my circle round you thrice
as if on honey dew I'd fed and drunk
the milk of paradise;

and again, at a seminar of critics
to appraise my woven bed-spread, and you
coming up to me amongst the people
urgently, urgently, how we need to
get to know each other heart to heart, and
I appalled, pull back; it was too public;

and we are talking together, colleagues,
an aesthetics seminar, and you ask

what we think the philosopher meant by
(phrase gone) and my saying with bold cliché
a form is a form because it cannot
take another shape; a cave or an urn
or cone; something about it containing
the shape of itself: a repetition
in the finite mind of the eternal
act of creation in the infinite
I Am. I am - the artist - transforming
himself in the act of transforming his
material. (Sic). Creative praxis.

Snakes in another dream, snakes and sisters
(the Queen and Princess Margaret, when they
were young, as my mother was, princesses);
what happened to the snakes I cannot tell -
but the Queen, persevering, declaiming
"I'm so glad you all came to the party";
and my writing, and the painting master
leaning over me, and it becomes clear
legible blue ballpoint printing transformed
to dense tapestry, a thickly textured
tree, naive, coarsly threaded, a child's tree
in the middle with a snake of fire like
thread weaving up the centre: and you, there,
standing over me, feeling the close stitch
of the brown background, meticulous,
muted hues; and your saying
how good it was.

The woman opens her eyes.
The afternoon sun reaches
round to them in the courtyard.
She looks at the child. She has
put down her pencils; the child
is curled on a grass mat; she
has brought an old receiving
blanket, spread it out to stop
the prickles. Her eyes are closed.
But is she weeping? Weak, weak,
the child is so weak; she lies
in the corner; tears trickle
like syrup, let her sleep then.

I too will close my eyes again.
Perhaps I shall see my painting,
perhaps its form will come to me.

"If poetry does not come as easily
as leaves to a tree it better not come at all."

Poetry like painting - gaps between the words -
ether in the interstices of the matter
(let the words rip, fiery threads along unseen
seams), measure the spaces between forms to give
the leaves shape; the tree, matter, life, what feels right.

The child wakes; they dress; they have tea and biscuits:

child: My Granny died before I was born.
woman: I know. I was with your Mum. Do you
      sometimes wish that you, too, had known her?
child: Yes. Of course. I miss her very much.
woman: When you think of her, how does she seem?
child: She is like a weeping willow, she
      is dressed in green; she is sitting, she
      has a thin foldy dress hanging down
      from her knees, she is turning away
      from me, I can't really see her face
      she has covered it with her hands.
woman: She was a wonderful woman.
child: That's what everyone says. Mummy says
      she would have loved me too; very much.
woman: Of course.
child: But she isn't here.
woman: No.

Come here, she says to the child
holding her arms to the child,
come here - child folding yourself
in my lap in mute grief - come here;
the woman is rocking her
holding her as if she were
her own; but these are not limbs
of her children; this is not
the sweaty hay-head of her
copper-curled boy, nor the fine
silver of her daughter, this

is a modest seal's head,
mute with nut-brown grief.

Do you believe in God, the child asks;
she hesitates, the woman, I don't
think so, no; Mummy says God
is dead; but we don't know, do we.

I am dreaming; I am five or six;
there is a picture of a warplane
in the paper my mother is reading,
holding me on her lap, soothing,
smoothing my hair, are we going to
die I ask and yes she answers yes.

There isn't a war here is there?
asks the child, and the woman thinks
of Folweni, the AKs, the
man who surrendered his taxi
his five hundred rand, then his life,
saying no, no here we are safe.

If perfect love is lost, dead,
can it rise somewhere again?

Dark man if I cannot will you here,
conjure you, I know I must meet you
at night: last night your limbs were ebony
black beautiful but you would not be
hurried to the wedding - last night he

gave me his strong soft arms but would not
be bound to me.
                    And then the engineer
saying the foundations built up there
on sand stone were suspect. What did he
want? The igneous rock, burst to the
surface form inside? How long could he wait?

The child shifts in the woman's lap;
they get up; move about the house
prepared, alert, shutting doors now -
they will go out - walk hand in hand
to Pigeon Valley; rest beside
the thick flutes of a muscled bole,
ovate viridifolia
cooling them, keeping them, at ease;
and when they come back there are eggs,
bath and bed.
                    The woman kisses
the child
                    as if she were her own.

Tomorrow we will go to the beach.
Night falls. Bats and crickets call.

She is ready to paint.
It will be "Self-portrait".

It will be of me, here in this room.
And the dark man shall be here, behind
me - the dark man, framed, hanging here too.

And the child, the child will be here too.
I will be turning back because she
will be calling - crouched in the front of
the frame, on the right, on the straw mat,
drawing, (the strong line from the top left -
the dark man, the picture hanging, then
to the middle, myself, to the right
the child; child holding out her picture
and my right hand stretched out, accepting.)

What symbols will announce you, dark man?
What will you look like, who shall you be?
In the picture of you (hanging in
my self portrait) you will be working;
carving out stone; strong arms abundant
with muscle, flesh like David's, your face
half turned toward me, aware I am
there; desire laconically spread
from your lowered lids (eyes to your work)

to your limbs working, working for me.
A wreath shall announce you - wreath of leaves
of yellow-wood and celtis, like the
wreath the children made at christmas time,
curled around the circle of your frame.

Now I see it; it is I who shall
be working. I shall be the painter
at work. In the painting I shall be
painting you - I shall not be intent
on the child, she will be there with her
magic giraffe, and I in profile,
dipping my brush and the painting I
am working on is you.

It will be
private, this picture, me painting here
in this room with the child; women and
children. The critics, then, may clamour
for the presence of the excluded;
raised voices clamouring at the gate;
I shall banish them; I shall get up
quietly, and shut the gate. I shall
take the phone off the hook.

I shall
call it not self-portrait but praxis
that will fox them work in progress come
let me see how I shall see you dark
man, how I shall be there working
to give you form, including the child.

She sets out her things. And as she works,
as the night gathers into deepest
dark, then begins to slip with the call

of early brown hooded kingfishers
into grey, his figure comes, clearly:
the long freckled back, the finely turned
legs, high instep, thin ankles, the pale
form, no phantom lover, familiar
maculate man, waking daily, here.

Behind him is his incomplete work;
his sculpture, his totem; carved around
its base are found the words "god of love".
His face is pale. There are rings under
his eyes.

      Around her painting she will
write, across the top - down the side -
along the bottom - up the side -
"where is the god of love to be found?"

Stone game

(i.m. Nancy Grenville d. 1994)

What can I learn about stories from you, Walcott,
and the craft of carving them for poems? Tender
poet, how your fingers feel for the face of your
childhood, trace its racing prints up the beach; benign
alien, returned to dusty streets, gathering
stones that dug warm bare feet.

                             You give it yourself your
youth your displacement you give us the stones in the
flesh like golden bread fruit softening the stabs.

Taking the embossed box from the chest of drawers we
lift the lid: jasper, agate, quartz, amethyst, turquoise,
tiger's-eye (semi-precious names learnt like a
litany from stones encased with the solid silver
of my mother's bracelet) we group in threes, my daughter
and I: spotted, striated, ochres; pinks, moss-greens, jades.

Fair head bent over our make-shift board, outside, under
the mango trees, she'll beat me to it: laughing at last
haul all the booty - gather the stones; Nancy's stone game.
(Far-away Nancy, my daughter's Granny's friend, from days
long gone, you brought the warmth of your youth, mothering, here.)
Now when we play I see traces of sticks in hot sand
squared for play - long-ago labourers at lunch playing
the game; mind drifting, fingers tracing stones, I see, too,

the game; mind drifting, fingers tracing stones, I see, too,
Nancy's sister's hair on end, the electric storm, and
little bare-foot Nancy, still hot with the shock, dancing
through the mangroves to the beach, next day, to tell her friends -
but she, my daughter, my quick silver fish, eyes only
for the present, for my moves, swallows my stones like bread.

How shall I trace it more clearly this connection -
youth, friendship, ocean crossings, stories, retracing past
prints in the sand, stones, stabbing the flesh, turned in the
hand to present mirth: across seas, crossed continents,
across generations, who shall I learn from, how?

Letter

Can I rouse myself to write this to you -
last night dreamt of - sleeping fleetingly -
weeks of unrest - heat - children struggling
for breath, rest, through me, rest - can I rise
note the heat rise from eyelids to ears
over breast, belly, licking the mount
of Venus and down to the dark bole -

that you cannot fill you never will
would not then - are you still then my what
will never stand erect be counted

come in come in come in -
                          (blue water -
sea - behind coral flame tree - slaking - sleep).

Symbol of Desire I could say
              you are for me, using the old words
the dead words, dead, begging the question,
              begging for me bereft, left bearing
the dread quick of this resurrected
              sweet St Theresa-like longing.

The dream: brushing your wife aside, kissing
you fierce and deep, claiming you, claiming what?
- a red herring linking me to real life -
this laat lammetjie, hesitation's child,

child of irrational desire, child
I know I have no strength for but long for,
this turning child, inside, here, would be born.

There are ways of reading your symbol;
Love or Writing - the elegiac
gesture - reaching after the always
inaccessible - meaning - present -
simply the soothing presence of words.

Lover of poetry - Wise One -
Father who will never quite send his
Spirit to me no matter how I beg -

But you: you the man: your long freckled
back, flame stoking articulate hands!

Words then; your word - body's substitute -
can you not even give me this? No
I could not fill you then because - no
I could not come to you because - no
I could not call you because because -
will you not even give me these? Look - I will
give them to you. Tell me -
                              yes I loved
you then all those years ago yes yes
I dream of you too still yes I longed
for you but you were too remote young
had too much to become; how could I give
myself to you saying here have me

I am here for you we need not look
any further we are here? Tell me
how could I? Tell me this.

                         Tell me. Write
me a letter a poem telling
why the dead are reborn. Is that what
I want to know? (how the dead rise up
intersticially, between the lines ...)
What then? Simply: is my dream burnt out
ashes for you?

                 See - writing the words,
the dead simple, dead end words I know
I can't carry this candle to you,
crossing seas to the dream world that you
belong to - dark currents churning flash
your bright features nightly; on a beach
stranded somewhere - last night - in the sun -
a book of poems, undamaged; see
the tide, the waves, the depth of the sea
having changed sharply, the book was safe -
and the message it held for you there
and my childish picture of a boat
you liked - against the odds - the poem
would get to you -

                  though you cannot lean
across the Styx, carry me, no, row
as I will, line by line, row by row,
line by line, shall I not reach you still?

Kissing the rod

"Sing to the ear that doth thy lays esteem
And gives thy pen both skill and argument.
Rise, resty Muse …." - Shakespeare

I am undoing your shirt
(I read your poems) you
are undoing mine

at least I think it is your
tremor on the buttons
asks do you want it

it must be for your beauty
(taken to bed with me) -
I am kissing your

buttons reaching reaching for
the point of no return
but see how little

I am you say kiss me kiss
me and I kiss the soft
shaft's rise - shall I leave

it at that - would it have stopped
there anyway - or tell
of feet in my back

kicking me to consciouness
the sharp every night nails
in the flesh - child's feet -

there's a moral here somewhere
only I can't get its
weak words anyway

the poet and the pen, the
interruption - being
found wanting - but o

the body of the dream I
would keep that obeisance
that   flesh rising

so what is this telling me
you have deserted me
you will desert me

you are always deserting me
word made flesh my king?
And what if woken

I cannot, do not resist the
dream - take for my needs take
you into me mouth

at my ear whispered words pressed
like limbs upon like seeds
within "take me here

I am here" and the woman
aroused arisen claims
alright alright I

am here to listen here lick
you into shape meaning
hard as it may be.

Sitting at home

"For us like any other fugitive,
it is today in which we live" - Auden

Sitting at home wanting to write like Auden
God help me
with a man in the roof over my head
fixing the rusty pipes

I'm here in the room outside wanting to write
God help me
like Auden: another man in my house
sanding, sealing the floors

he's laying the groundwork for easy cleaning
God help us
keep passages aseptic asthmatic
air-pipes clear: wanting to

write: a romantic modernist metaphor
for God's sake
for work writing tell me what should I do
since what I want to do

is write about writing and about wanting
God knows why
to write. This is the same day I want to
remind myself firmly

gently enough is enough you have managed
God knows how
enough, having seen children to school food
in their tummies clean clothes

on their backs anxious airways unclogged enough
thank God - breathe -
despite the outside room the broken pipes
despite the tacky floors

today is the day I tell myself we can't
for God's sake
all write like Auden under the circum-
stances under the roof

with the man in it today is the day I
o my God
receive the manuscript returned today
is the day I could lie

at the table banging my head on the wood
God help me
I want the mellifluous density
of Auden the thickness

of thought in true song dour like dough sour
like age flesh
on the bones of the verses risen life
in the soul of the words.